LAST STOP

They see the things we can't...

WATCHERS

WATCHERS

LAST STOP

PETER LERANGIS

AN
APPLE
PAPERBACK

SCHOLASTIC INC.
New York Toronto London Auckland Sydney

ISBN 0-590-10996-0

12 11 10 9 8 7 6 5 4 3 2   8 9/9 1 2 3/0

Printed in the U.S.A.   40

First Scholastic printing, November 1998

To George Nicholson, who brought the idea to life;
Herb Strean, who provided a place for it to grow;
David Levithan, who gave it wings;
And, always, Tina, Nick, and Joe, who give it meaning.

LAST STOP

WATCHERS
Case File: 3583

Name: David Moore

Age: 13

First contact: 33.35.67

Acceptance:

He's not ready.

1

Here's what I remember most:
Heat.

You could see it rising from the pavement in waves.

Humidity.

It slid off your skin, like hot oil off a skillet.

Anger.

Mine. At everything.

Mostly at my friends — Heather, Max, and Clarence. They'd talked me into riding the subrail home. On the last day of the work week. When all the Franklin City municipal workers leave their offices early — exactly when we middle-school kids leave classes.

I hate crowds. I hardly ever ride the sub.

On this day each week, my dad used to give me a ride in a squad car. He worked for the city, too. He was a case solver in the Public Guardian Department.

But I hadn't had any rides home in six months. So there I was, standing shoulder to shoulder, dripping wet, on the putrid-smelling platform of the Booker Street station. Which leads to the other major reason I was angry.

Dad.

In fact, Dad was all I ever thought about. In class. At home. Whenever the voicephone rang. I'd picture him, and all I wanted to do was scream.

Which wasn't fair, really.

For one thing, he was a nice guy. I loved him.

For another thing, he was dead.

Six months earlier, he'd left my mom and me. He got out of bed, dressed himself, and kissed Mom good-bye. When she asked where he was going, all he said was "Home."

He never came back.

Dad was already totally off his konker by then. It had started with headaches, about a year and a half ago. Then sudden blackouts at odd times. Soon he was forgetting simple things. Talking baby talk. Taking walks and ending up in some stranger's swimming pool in a neighboring town. Doctors checked him for everything — blood clots, tumors, Fassbinder's disease. They thought it might be inherited, but Dad had no family records at all. He was an orphan and didn't even know where his parents had come from.

Whenever Dad strayed, Mom called the pugs, the good old Public Guardians. They would always bring him back. They were Dad's loyal buddies.

But this time, the pugs came up empty-handed. They contacted other departments in suburbs nearby. Eventually the search spread to include the whole country. A reward was posted for anyone who sighted Dad.

Soon the radio call-in shows started. The TV talk shows.

Tons of people thought they had seen him. Fishing in the Palm Tree Lakes. Moose hunting. Heading a religious cult. Hiding in a cave.

But every lead checked out false.

Mom tried to be optimistic. She began going to this therapy group. (She thought I should, too, but I said *no way*.)

For weeks, I didn't sleep. Whenever I closed my eyes, I saw Dad. Walking into my room. Sitting at the foot of the bed. Smiling.

Then my eyes would pop open. And he'd be gone.

I tried to believe that Dad was alive. But that made me feel horrible. Because if he *were* alive, that meant he didn't want to see us. Or he didn't remember us. Or worse.

When the pugs gave up, I knew it was all over. I could tell by the way they looked at me, all soft and pitying. If Dad had been found, we'd have known about it. His face had been broadcast coast-to-coast.

I tried to forget. I plunged into homework, chores, school activities — all so I wouldn't have time to think of him.

The worst part? He hadn't said good-bye to me. In dreams *I* would say that to him, over and over. But he'd just smile.

I kept seeing him everywhere. In shadows and shop aisles. In ball fields and on bikes.

He'd left me. But he wasn't leaving me alone.

So the anger crept in. And grew.

As I stood at the subrail station, the feelings were balling up in my head. Like a fist.

Sweat prickled my neck. My shirt was soaked. I knew that when I got home, Mom would make me take a shower. We had to appear on a local TV show that afternoon. To talk about Dad, of course.

I hated those shows. I hated being an object of pity. Answering dumb questions.

And to make matters worse, my friends were acting like total idiots. Giggling. Making fart noises.

I stepped away. And I saw a familiar figure. To my right. A man in a blue shirt, trudging down the subrail stairs, face buried in a newspaper.

Dad.

My heart jumped. I spun to face him.

Then he put the paper down. And my eyes locked with those of an ashen-faced, annoyed stranger.

Again.

How many times had this happened? A hundred?

And each time as painful as the last.

I felt pressure behind my eyelids.

Tears.

I was not going to cry. I'd vowed not to. For six long months I had kept it in.

The crowd on the platform thickened. I could hear a distant rumbling. I leaned over the edge and saw two pinpoints of light approaching in the tunnel darkness.

The train screeched into the station. The cars were already packed. Everyone behind us began to shove as the door opened.

A sudden memory. I'm running to catch the train with Dad. I'm five years old. Dad races ahead and reaches the car door first. He turns to face me, holding out his arms and legs in an X-shape. The door begins to close on him and I scream. I scream because I think he is going to die . . .

Stop.

I had to stop thinking.

Heather and Clarence squeezed in first.

Max and I made it just as the door slid closed on our backs.

Heather could barely reach the handrail above her head. Next to her a sweaty bearded guy was holding a newspaper in her face.

The man next to me must have had slugs with garlic for lunch. The odor was knocking me out.

As the train picked up speed, I turned away. Now I was facing the door. I stared blankly through the window, trying to hold my breath. I felt sick.

Then the train stopped.

Cold. In the tunnel.

The overhead fluorescents blinked off. Instantly the car was pitch-black. Muffled groans rose all around me.

Claustrophobia.

I felt icy cold. I couldn't see the bodies around me but I heard them. Breathing loud, like bandsaws. Breathing-machines. Closing in on me . . .

Where were we?

Between the Booker and Deerfield Street stops.

11

Granite Street.

I remembered. The old, abandoned station. It was here, somewhere. We used to watch for it when we were kids. The long platform lit by three bare lightbulbs. The grimy tiles spelling out "Granite." The yellowed, graffiti-covered walls. The floor with a carpet of dust.

Look for it.

Yes. Keep my mind off the claus

off the

Lights.

Lights?

Outside the window.

The platform, the walls, the floor. Gleaming. Like a movie set.

Yes. They filmed down here. Often.

But they couldn't have set it up so fast.

I rubbed my eyes. I blinked.

Claustrophobia. Panic. Visions.

Still there.

Ads cried out from the walls. Movies I'd never heard of. Odd names. Phrases that made no sense, like "us open."

People, too. Dozens. Dressed in funny clothes. Not ugly, just . . . off. The colors, the cut of the pants, the lengths of the skirts.

Off.

On the walls, a mosaic of purple tiles spelled out the name of the station.

86TH STREET.

No. "Granite." It was Granite Street.

The people on the platform were moving now. Toward the middle door of the car. Kids squealed, looking into

The car.

In the car, it was pitch-black. I felt bodies, I heard the breathing. But I saw no one. Despite the brightness outside the window.

How?

None of the station's light was penetrating inside. As if it were being absorbed and reflected at the same time.

I opened my mouth to say something — anything.

Then, a sudden *whoosh*. To my right.

The middle door of the car slid open. Through it poured

Light?

It was more than bright, somehow. *Loud* light. Solid.

A box of light.

Now I could see the passengers around me.

13

I looked for the shock in their faces. The recognition that I wasn't alone.

But all I saw was boredom. Annoyance. As if nothing had happened.

From among them, a man jostled into the light. A familiar man. I'd seen him on the train before, one of those thin, droopy people who always seem sad and afraid.

He clutched a small sky-blue business card. He cringed in the glare. But he was grinning.

The people on the platform let out a welcoming cheer. The man blinked. Eyes adjusting, he stepped through the door. His cheeks were streaked with tears.

The crowd swallowed him up, patting him on the back, hugging him, kissing him. He almost lost his cap. His business card floated to the ground.

Then the door closed. Again, blackness inside.

The train lurched forward, then stopped. The overhead lights flickered on, harsh and greenish-white.

"We are experiencing difficulty . . ." blared the conductor's voice over the speakers.

The train began to move. The overhead lights winked, then went off again.

I kept my eyes on the station. The jubilant crowd was now leading the man up a flight of stairs. Except for one person. One man standing alone, peering at our train.

A scream caught in my throat. I grabbed at the rubber pads between the door and tried to yank them open, even though the car was moving.

That was when my father saw me. And he waved, until the train rolled out of sight.

Sometimes it just has to happen.
And that makes you ready.

2

*D*ad.

The word exploded in my brain.

It couldn't be.

But it *was*. It was Dad. He'd seen me.

My dad was alive.

SMMMACK! SMMMACK! SMMMACK!

I was banging on the door with my fists now.

"WAIT!"

My own voice, piercing and raw.

People were staring at me now. The guy with the garlic breath edged away. His face looked curdled. His eyes were darting nervously from me to the window.

The station was out of sight. Grimy subrail walls sped by, illuminated by the dull glow of an occasional lightbulb.

"Next stop, Deerfield!" the conductor's voice blared over the speakers.

A dream.

Is it possible to have dreams when you're wide-awake?

Of course.

Stress. That's what it was.

Stress was making me see things. Like the guy in the blue shirt.

Maybe I was going crazy.

My friends definitely thought so. I could see that in their stunned expressions.

The train was slowing again as we approached the Deerfield Street station. One stop short of my own.

I felt humiliated. I had to get out. I was close enough to walk the rest of the way home, no pain.

When the doors opened, I slipped out. I sped through the station at a dead run, took the stairs three at a time, and dashed outside into daylight. Bright, clear daylight.

I was running across Deerfield at the corner of Orpheus when I heard a familiar voice cry out, "David!"

Heather. What was she doing here?

Honnnnnnk!

A car swerved by me, its brakes squealing.

I jumped back, colliding with a streetlight.

Heather raced up to me. "Are you okay?"

No. I couldn't tell her. It was crazy. I needed to be alone.

"Fine," I grunted, turning away. "See you."

"David, what is wrong with you?" Heather asked.

"Nothing!" I snapped. "Why are you following me around?"

"Uh, I live in your building, remember? I have to walk in this direction."

"You didn't have to get off a stop early."

"Excuse me for being concerned? I just saw the quietest guy I know — you — banging on a subrail door and screaming like a maniac. So, being your friend, I ran after you, just in

21

time to save your life from a speeding motorist, and this is the thanks I get?"

What luck. Just when I need privacy, a little bonding time with my sanity, I am tailed by the motormouth of Franklin City Middle School.

"It was a joke," I said.

"Yelling 'wait' to the empty subrail track?"

"To shake up the commuters. Make them think I'm a total filbert, so they'll move away and give me room."

"Liar."

I turned in the direction of Wiggins Street, toward home.

"Face it, David," came Heather's voice behind me. "You need to talk. You're having a tough time . . . I mean, psychologically, with your dad and all — "

I stopped in my tracks. *What does my dad have to do with it?"*

"Nothing . . . I'm just saying . . . you haven't been yourself since . . . you know . . ."

"So isn't that *my* business? Isn't it my business if I'm stressed out and seeing things and needing time alone?"

"Seeing things? Like what?"

"You really want to know? You want to be my shrink? Okay, Heather — *like my dad!* On subrail platforms, on the street, at the Granite Street station! Okay? Happy?"

Stop.

What was I saying?

I wanted to reel in the words. I wanted to disappear. I wanted to put my life into reverse, go back to school, and never go near the subrail system again.

But I couldn't. And Heather was not going to let this go away.

"You saw *your dad*?"

I felt nauseated now. Smothered. As if the street noises had been sucked away, leaving only the sounds of my brain, churning and rumbling like an oncoming train.

I saw nothing but Heather's eyes, looming closer.

"I'm listening, David. Go on." She was touching my hand now. Half of me wanted to recoil, but I felt my fingers gripping hers.

I did go on. I told her everything, all the details. Hoping that would ease the pain and confusion I felt.

Heather looked stone-faced at me the

whole time. When I was done, she leaned back against the wall of a building and sighed. "Who-o-oa . . ."

"You have to promise not to tell anyone," I said. "Ever."

Heather nodded.

"I know, I know. You think I'm crazy."

"No, I don't . . ." Heather said softly.

"You don't?"

"I just have one question. How much sleep are you getting?"

"What does that have to do with anything?"

"I read somewhere that you need a lot more sleep when you reach adolescence. Which could possibly be happening to you. I mean, it's a difficult time of life, especially for guys. Look how it warped Max — "

She didn't believe me. I wanted to kill her.

I ran off and let her babble to herself.

When I reached our apartment building, she was nowhere near me. I stepped inside, walked across the vestibule, and pressed the elevator button. The number 12 lit up on the metal plate above the door.

That's where the elevator was. Twelve. Top

floor. By the time it came down, Heather would be waiting beside me.

I decided to take the stairs to my apartment, which is on the fifth floor. The building's stairwell is behind a locked metal door, opposite the elevator. I ran toward it, fumbling for my keys.

With a loud *ca-chunk*, the door flew open, clipping my arm.

A man with a greasy beard and a long, ragged coat leaped out.

I can't watch this.

We have to be ready, too. For anything.

3

"AAAAAAGGGGGH!" I screamed.

"AAAAAAAGGGGGH!" he screamed.

I shot back against the wall.

The man stood, stoop-shouldered, staring at me. His rank smell filled the entire vestibule.

I recognized the smell before the face.

Anders. Anders the Mad Hermit of Wiggins Street.

"You scared me," I said.

Anders giggled. I could see his missing front tooth.

His hair was stringy and matted, not to mention his clothes. It looked as if he hadn't bathed or changed or cut his hair since . . . well, since Dad started going off the deep end.

I felt kind of sad. Dad was always doing stuff for Anders — visiting him occasionally, helping him clean up his apartment, running errands. Why? Because Dad loved everyone, including total filberts, I guess. Dad used to insist that Anders was once a normal guy. Which was kind of hard to imagine.

Dad used to be Anders's connection to reality. Now *Anders* was the one sane enough to still be alive.

How ironic.

"Excuse me," I said, pushing past Anders.

"Has . . . he . . . come . . . back?" he growled.

"Who?"

"Your papa!"

"Uh, no," I replied. "He's . . . well, gone."

Anders's beard moved, which I took to be a smile. "To 'the undiscovered country, from whose bourn no traveler returns.' "

"You could say that, I guess. Whatever."

"Are you sure?" Now Anders was glaring.

"Well . . . yeah. I guess. I mean — "

Ding!

The elevator opened behind me. I glanced at the door. No Heather.

"Talk to Mom about it!" I blurted out as I backed in.

Hallelujah. Escape.

I rode up to the fifth floor and went straight to my apartment. Swinging the door open, I threw my backpack into the living room.

As usual, it landed on the sofa.

As not usual, my mom caught it.

Her hair had been set into curls, and she was wearing makeup. "Where have you been? Don't tell me. You used dial-a-turtle to get home. You know, we have to be at the studio in *fifteen minutes.*"

The show. I had totally forgotten about the show. The Sophie Karp talk show.

"Sorry," I muttered.

Bleeeeeep! went the voicephone.

"Go transform yourself into a prince." Mom snatched up the receiver. "Hello? . . . Yes, this is she . . . Where? No, he doesn't . . . Well, okay, thank you very much."

Mom groaned as she hung up.

"Who was that?" I asked.

"Woman. Old. From a place called Talmadge Swamp. Saw Dad's photo in a tabloid and swears she spotted him alligator hunting. *Now hurry. I am leaving!*"

Zoom. Into the bathroom. I showered quickly, wrestled my hair with a comb, and tucked in my shirt.

We sped downtown in an ancient taxi that sounded like pneumonia on wheels. The driver cursed every time he hit a pothole, which was about four times a block.

I didn't mind. I would have been happy on a camel. *Anything* besides the subrail.

By the time we reached TFCT, Franklin City's local TV station, my stomach was fluttery with nerves. Once inside, Mom and I were whisked away to a makeup room, where three or four people fussed over us. It felt kind of cool, until I saw the final result.

My hair was all puffed up and hard as a helmet. The hairspray was making my eyes itch. And I was wearing eyeliner and rouge.

I looked like an idiot.

Next thing I knew, Mom and I were sitting

on the living room set of *The Sophie Karp Show*. And Sophie Karp was smiling at us, talking a mile a minute.

I have no idea what she said. All I remember is that *she* looked great — killer smile, friendly face, great hair.

The lights blinked on. White. Harsh. Glaring. The theme music began. The studio audience broke into applause.

I was shaking. My stomach felt like the inside of a cement mixer.

"Today we meet a courageous family," Sophie Karp said as the music died down, "a mother and son on a mission of faith. Six months ago, in the middle of the night . . ."

Dad. In my nervous state, the images were flooding in. The train grinding to a stop. The lights . . .

". . . and now," Sophie Karp went on in a hushed, dramatic voice, "when Taylor Moore and her son meet in the kitchen each morning for breakfast, they must remind themselves not to put that third strip of bacon . . ."

The blood was rushing from my face.

". . . not to scramble up that extra egg . . ."

Keep calm . . .

". . . and I know it's a lot of stress for a twelve-year-old, isn't it?"

Now the audience was staring at me.

I turned. Sophie Karp was to my left. Her microphone was in my face.

"Uh, thirteen." My voice squeaked on the "teen." Great.

The audience laughed. I felt about two inches tall.

Sophie Karp made some dumb joke, then her face grew serious again. "Every year, thousands disappear, never to be heard of again . . ."

Mom gripped my hand.

"Are they all dead?" Sophie Karp continued solemnly. "Not so, says our next guest."

Guest? Who had said anything about a guest?

"Will you please welcome . . . Gardenia Rouelle-Savant!"

The curtain behind us opened and the audience clapped loudly. In walked a woman about six feet tall, wearing a silk turban and a long, flowing dress. She took a slow bow, her face solemn and dark.

As she walked to us, she seemed to be floating. She sat grandly in a chair to Mom's right, then leaned over and folded one hand over mine and another over Mom's, as if we were old friends. She greeted us with a deep, accented "Helllllooo."

I felt as if lizards were racing up my spine. I did not like this. Not at all.

"Ms. Rouelle-Savant's book, *The World Unseen,* has been on best-seller lists for months," Sophie Karp announced. "She specializes in mysterious disappearances and the life in the hereafter . . ."

I gave Mom a glance. She looked like someone under attack.

Gardenia Rouelle-Savant's eyes were closed tightly. "Yesssss," she moaned. "Ohhhh, yes."

People would be *watching* this. My heart was sinking.

"What is it?" Sophie Karp asked. "Do you feel something? Do you know something that will help these people?"

Gardenia Rouelle-Savant let go of Mom and held out her hand toward Sophie Karp, as if to say *Be quiet.*

"Alan," she whispered. "Alan Moore? Is that his name?"

Mom nodded warily.

"He's here," said the woman.

The audience gasped.

Sophie Karp looked around. "Here *in our studio?*"

"No," Gardenia Rouelle-Savant replied gravely. "In a world that coexists with ours. A world that very few of us can see, I'm afraid . . . only those with the sight."

A few giggles broke out in the audience.

Gardenia Rouelle-Savant's eyes slowly opened. They turned toward Mom briefly, then rested on me like dark sunbeams. "And you have it," she said softly. "Don't you, young man?"

Phony. She's a phony.

I knew it, but it didn't matter. Those eyes were spearing me. I felt light-headed. Freezing cold.

"David?" Mom whispered. "Are you okay?"

He was waiting. He was sane and breathing and happy and waiting for me.

The entire studio seemed to be disappearing in white light, all except the face of Gardenia Rouelle-Savant.

"May I be excused?" I asked.

I didn't wait for an answer. I stood up and ran toward the men's room.

Behind me, I could hear the voice of Sophie Karp. "I — I'm sorry. This is a very emotional segment, folks. We'll have to take a station break. When we come back . . ." *Sniff, sniff.* ". . . men who love women who love their jobs more than men who don't. Stay tuned."

She's trouble.

He's gone.

4

"You look awful on TV," Heather said.

"Thanks," I replied.

Clack-clackety-clack-clack went Heather's fingers on her computer keyboard.

The words SUBRAIL, FRANKLIN CITY slowly appeared on the screen. Heather clicked on "Search" and sat back.

CONNECTING . . . a message flashed.

Outside Heather's window, the sixth-day-morning dog walkers were heading for the park. They looked as bleary-eyed as I felt.

Heather's parents were asleep in the next

room. Her baby brother was asleep, too. *I should have been asleep, recovering from the Sophie Karp show the day before.* But no. Heather had to call and apologize, then insist I come over.

And I had been stupid enough to accept.

"Uh, why are we doing this?" I asked.

Heather ignored the question. "You should be excited. I mean, if someone told me *I* could see into parallel worlds — "

"I can barely see *our* world at this hour."

"Click on, David. Gardenia Whatever is famous. What if she's right? Haven't you read any science fiction?"

"Those are stories, Heather. This is real life. That woman is a fake. She doesn't have a license or a degree or anything."

"Then how did she know your dad's first name?"

"She could have looked it up in the directory."

"And how did she know you saw him in that train station?"

"She didn't *know*! All she said was — "

Heather wasn't listening. A list of sites had popped onto the screen. Heather scrolled down, then clicked on one of the titles: "Abandoned Treasures: Stations of the Past."

An article appeared instantly. Heather skimmed through it, then stopped.

"Listen to this." She began to read: " 'Thirty years ago, at the height of the city's financial trouble, several stations were discontinued rather suddenly' . . . blah blah blah . . . 'Passengers who used the Granite Street station were appalled one morning to arrive at their familiar entrance, only to see a freshly cemented sidewalk.' Aha! That's it!"

"That's what?"

"Don't you get it? *Thirty years ago.* It's a rip in time! You were looking back into the past, David!"

Groaning, I launched myself onto Heather's bed. It hit the wall with a thump. "You called me on a weekend morning, woke me in the middle of a dream, and made me come over here *for your stupid science fiction ideas?*"

" 'Nowadays the stations lie moldering,' " Heather read on, " 'used on occasion as storage space and movie sets.' "

"There you go," I said. "A movie set. *That's* what I saw."

"Uh, right, David. A movie set visible only to you. *The Vanishing Mole People of Granite Street.*"

The image replayed itself in my mind for about the millionth time. But something stood out. Something I hadn't really paid attention to.

I sat up suddenly. "It wasn't Granite Street."

"Yes, it was, David — "

"No! The sign on the wall. It didn't *say* Granite Street. It was something else. A numbered street."

Heather looked at me skeptically. "That's ridiculous. Why would it have said that?"

"You're asking me? The whole *thing* is ridiculous — it was a hallucination!"

"Unless, years ago, the station had another name . . ." Heather began clacking away at the computer again. "Like when the city was first founded . . ."

"They didn't have subrails back then!"
BLEEEEEEEEP!

Saved by Heather's voicephone.

She leaped across the room and picked it up. "Hello? . . . You *what*? . . . Get out of here! . . ." Heather's eyes were darting nervously toward me. "Both of you? . . . What were you doing down there? . . . Oh my God. . . . Okay. We'll be right down."

Heather slammed down the receiver and headed for her door. "Come on. We're out of here."

I tagged close behind. "Wait! Where are we going?"

"To the subrail," Heather replied, grabbing a coat from a hook in the front closet. "It looks like you're not the only one who has the sight, David. Clarence saw it, too."

Clarence?

Curious.

5

I panted for breath as we ran down Wiggins Street. "Are you sure they were serious?"

"I will be *so-o-o-o-o* angry if I'm not able to see this thing," Heather said through clenched teeth.

"What are they doing down there on a weekend morning, anyway?" I pressed on.

"It figures, doesn't it? I'm probably the only one of us who doesn't have the sight — "

"And why did they just happen to call *you*? And why are they still down there?"

Heather glanced my way, as if she just now

noticed me. "Clarence is kind of freaked out, and he won't stop pacing the platform. He wants to go back and take the ride again, just to be sure. Max remembered what you had seen — "

"How could he remember? I never told him!"

"I did."

I stopped running. I felt as if I'd been punched in the stomach.

"This was supposed to be a secret, Heather!"

"Sorry," Heather said, turning toward me. "I only told Max, though. And I didn't mention the part about your father — "

"But you promised!"

"Don't be a baby, David. This is important."

"And a promise to me *isn't*?"

Heather rolled her eyes. "We are talking about a major psychic phenomenon, okay? I guarantee, this cannot stay a secret for long. You will be needing a press agent soon."

"And I guess *you* want the job!"

"I will ignore that remark. Instead, like a good friend I will politely answer the question you asked me. For your information, Max called *your* house first. Your mom found the note you left, and she told them you were with me. Max and Clarence and the others were on the way home from an early strike-ball game downtown. Any other questions?"

"Heather, I don't want to have anything to do with this!"

"Fine. Good-bye."

Heather disappeared down the station stairs.

I glowered at her for a moment.

Then, grumbling, I followed.

Max and Clarence were waiting just inside the rotary gates. So were three other kids from our class, all in strikeball uniforms — Cheryl Howard, Rod Skinner, and Lenny Feldman. All of them looked a little shell-shocked.

"Oh, great," I murmured as I caught up with Heather. "It's turning into a party. Soon the whole school will know."

"I said I was sorry," Heather hissed.

I inserted a token into the rotary gate and pushed my way through. "Listen, you guys, if this is some kind of joke — "

"Did you *all* see it?" Heather asked.

Max shook his head. "Just Clarence."

"He wants to go back," Lenny said. "With witnesses this time. As many as possible."

Rod Skinner circled his index finger around his ear in a *cuckoo* gesture. Max immediately poked him in the side.

"Oh. No offense, Moore," Rod said.

"David, maybe you can get through to him," Max said. "We can't. He just shut off."

"Talk to him," Heather whispered.

They were all looking at me now. With concern.

I approached Clarence. He didn't seem to notice me. He was pacing the floor, looking up the track, and muttering, "Come on . . . come on, baby."

In the distance, I could hear the oncoming train. "Clarence?" I said.

"Leave me alone!" He snapped around angrily. But his face instantly softened. "Oh, it's you . . ."

A joke. He's playing a joke. "Uh, Clarence, can you tell me exactly what you saw?"

He shrank into himself, looking off into the distance. "This light . . . I mean, I guess it was light . . . but how . . . ?"

Cheryl was behind me now. "He said it was bright out there, but the inside of the car was pitch-black."

How could he have known that detail? Had I told that to Heather?

"Clarence, were there people on the platform?" I pressed.

Clarence nodded. "The door opened. And someone on the train — a kid — he stepped out. And they were so happy to see him."

I braced myself for the question I had to ask. "Did you see . . . anyone you recognized?"

WHO-O-O-O-O-ONK! With a loud horn blast, the train pulled into the station.

We all turned to one another.

"Uh, Clarence," Lenny said, "you sure you don't want to go home . . ."

"Get some rest . . ." Rod continued.

The train was stopping now, its brakes shrieking. "No," Clarence said. "We have to go."

Heather gave me a look. A *see-I-told-you-so* look.

She boarded the train after Clarence. Then Max, Rod, Cheryl, and Lenny.

I tried to move my legs but they wouldn't

go. The thought of taking the trip again was paralyzing me.

Heather stood in the door, holding it open. "Well?"

"I — I have to think about this — " I stammered.

Heather yanked me inside by the arm.

The doors whooshed closed. The car was empty except for a man in a down coat sleeping on one of the bench seats. Lenny, Cheryl, Max, and Rod were already kneeling on another seat, staring out the window.

Clarence was by the door, gripping a handrail. His jaw was set, his face grim. Heather stood next to him. "Tell me when you see it," she whispered.

The train began to roll, picking up speed. It stopped at Deerfield, then went on.

My legs started to shake.

Then the Granite Street station was coming into view. Dim and grimy and empty. But the train was not slowing down.

We were going to pass right by.

EEEEEEEEE . . .

Squealing brakes.

The train lurched violently, then stopped.

I tumbled to the floor.

Then, blackness. No light whatsoever. I could feel Heather next to me, sprawled on the floor.

And Clarence started screaming.

But we were told not to interfere.

It may not work if we don't.

6

I tried to scramble to my feet, but my legs were tangled with Heather's.

"Get off me!" I shouted.

"You get off me!" Heather cried.

"AAAAAAAGHHHH!" Clarence repeated.

Heather grabbed my shoulders. I grabbed hers. We both struggled to stand up.

My blood pounded. I was scared. Scared of seeing Dad's face. Scared that I wouldn't see it. Scared that I wouldn't know what to do. That the train would pull away before I could decide.

I forced myself to look out the window.

My heart stopped beating. Stopped cold.

A sooty floor. A few lightbulbs. Broken tiles. Nothing else.

"What the — ?" I said.

I don't know who started laughing first. Max, I think.

Then Cheryl let out a snort. And before long, everyone but Heather was whooping like a hyena. Cracking up. I could see their silhouettes in the darkness, bobbing up and down.

"And the Best Actor Award goes to Clarence Mitchell!" Max hooted.

"You guys are sick," Heather rasped.

"Not bad, huh?" Clarence said.

This is not happening.

A setup. The whole thing had been a setup.

And the worst part? I had seen it coming, and I *still* fell for it.

I looked from one hysterical, mocking face to the next.

I couldn't take it. All the bottled-up tension, all the uncertainty and anger exploded.

I lunged at Clarence.

"Hey!" he cried out, falling onto a seat. "It was just a joke!"

"You ever do that again, I will kill you!" I shouted.

SMMMMACK!

The door between the cars slid open. My eyes had adjusted enough to the dark to see a subrail officer barreling toward us. "Which one of you pulled the emergency brake?"

So *that* was how they had stopped the train.

"He did it!" said Clarence, pointing to Max.

"Did not!" Max protested. "I was *here*. Lenny did it!"

No one would admit to it. I slumped against the nearest car door, and Heather slumped next to me.

"What a pack of jerks," she said.

"You should talk," I shot back. "This wouldn't have happened if you hadn't opened your big mouth."

"*I* didn't ask them to do this!" Heather insisted. "I *told* Max not to tell anyone."

"Great, Heather. That's like telling a dog not to bark."

"It's hard to keep something this important inside, David. Look, *you're* the one who has this . . . this *power.* Maybe if you opened up, if you didn't try to keep it a secret, this kind of thing wouldn't happen."

"I am not hearing this."

"Be proud of yourself, David. This could be, like, the discovery of a new dimension — "

"You want to see a new dimension? Look out the window, Heather! You are seeing exactly what I see. No people. No signs. No lights. Nothing!"

"But yesterday — "

"Yesterday I was seeing things! The train was crowded, I was thinking about my dad — it was *stress*, okay? I'm over it. But now you have to go turn it into some big — "

The words caught in my throat. To my left, I was vaguely aware of my so-called friends still arguing with the subrail officer.

But my eyes were focused on something outside the window. Something on the floor of the old station.

A sky-blue business card.

Oh.

No.

1

"I'm sorry, all right?" Heather was saying. "I'll make it up to you — "

"Heather — " I whispered.

"I'm really not a bad person, David. I just — "

"Heather, look out the window!"

Heather's face went slack. "What? Oh my God, David, are you having . . . the *sight?*"

"No. There!" I pointed.

"The card?"

"Yes!"

Heather gave me a look. "So?"

"*So*, remember? The guy I told you about, in my hallucination? The one who left the train? He was holding a business card that same color, *and he dropped it!*"

Even in the near-darkness, I could see Heather's eyes glow. "Oh, David. Oh, this is big. Very big."

"I mean, it could just be, like, some trash," I said. "Plenty of people throw stuff out the window — "

"David, you have to get that card."

"How am I supposed to do that?"

"I don't know. Ask the pug?"

"He's about to put us all in jail!"

"Um . . . a long pole with chewgum at the end?"

"Big help."

To our left, the pug was still arguing with our friends. To my right, a few irate passengers were barging through the door that led from the next car. Right past the sign that said DO NOT ENTER OPEN AREA BETWEEN CARS.

Open area.

That was it.

I stood up. "Cover me," I whispered to Heather.

As I ran toward the far end of the car, Heather was right behind me. I could tell she was complaining, but I couldn't make out her words over the commotion.

I grabbed the metal handle and pulled. The door slid open with a dull *thunk*.

Cold, musty air rushed into the car. I stepped through the opening. Just outside the door was a metal ledge, wide enough for one person. It curved in a semicircle around me, and I could see over it to the black chasm of the track bed below.

"I'll wait here," Heather whispered.

"Thanks, braveheart," I replied.

As my eyes adjusted to the blackness, I scanned the platform. Soot had gathered as thick as a snowfall. Barely detectable footsteps led to a graffiti-smeared tile wall. Small piles of trash lay strewn about, most of it blackened by grime.

I can't.

"What are you waiting for?" Heather hissed.

"It's disgusting!" I said.

"You have shoes on!"

"No kidding. What if the train starts to move?"

"It won't. The emergency brake shuts down the electricity for the whole line. It takes forever to start up again."

I spotted the sky-blue card. It was to my left, near the center of the car. A short walk. An easy walk.

I stepped over the chasm. I planted my foot on the platform. It felt slippery.

Next foot.

I was completely off the train now. I turned to my left and started walking slowly.

A squeaky noise. A skittering in the shadows.

I froze up.

Rats.

I hate rats.

Hold on.

The card was within reach. I leaned down and picked it up.

"David!" Heather's voice called out.

SMMMMACK!

The sound of the sliding metal door startled me.

"HEY! KID!"

I turned. The glare of a flashlight blinded me.

Behind the light, I could make out the shape of the subrail pug. He was leaping onto the platform, heading right for me. "WHAT DO YOU THINK YOU'RE DOING?"

Just what I was asking myself.

I backed away.

My right foot slid on the grime. Windmilling my arms, I fell face first.

I hit the floor with a muffled thud.

Grit flew into my mouth. My eyes stung. I started coughing like crazy.

Out of the corner of my eye, I could see my friends peering out the window of the car. Dumbfounded.

A hand gripped my shoulder and turned me around.

I was facing a holstered gun.

"Young man," the guardian said, "you are under arrest."

We've lost him.

8

"And I want to make clear," said the chief subrail guardian, pacing his office, "that pulling the emergency brake recklessly and trespassing on FCSS property are *both* misdemeanors — "

I sat forward in my seat. "But I didn't pull the brake — "

"And *both* are punishable by law!" the chief boomed.

Mom was glowering at me. She looked angry, but her eyes were all teary and her lips were starting to quiver.

"I understand," I muttered.

I was a criminal.

A *filthy* criminal. The soot I'd fallen into was like paint. If I wiped it, it just spread. The chief had to put a plastic cover on the seat before I could sit on it.

My future passed through my mind: a small cell . . . ankle chains . . . dates checked off on a stone wall . . .

"What — what's going to happen to him?" Mom asked.

"Juvenile court is the usual step," the chief replied.

"But he's never done anything wrong before!" Mom pleaded.

The chief walked behind his desk, sat down, and sighed deeply. "Son, I knew your dad. His department worked with ours. He was a good man. You must miss him."

I bowed my head. Mom choked back a sniffle.

"I'm going to let you go," the chief went on. "But with the strongest possible warning. What you did was not only illegal but extremely dangerous."

I nodded.

"Thank you," Mom said.

The chief nodded. "Now go home and take a good bath, young man."

Mom was not in a cheery mood as we left the FCSS headquarters.

"Do you know how lucky you were just now? Don't you *ever* do something stupid like that again. Why were you on that train? Who gave you permission to leave the house?"

"Mom, I'm thirteen — "

"So that means you're free to go out and disrupt the entire subrail system?" She was practically screaming.

"I told you I didn't *do* that!"

"You could have been killed!"

"I know!"

"I've already lost *one*. Do I really need to lose you, too? Because of your own stupidity?"

Enough. I had had enough.

Enough of being yelled at. Laughed at. Framed for something I didn't do.

"*I'm not stupid!*" I shouted. "I only went out there because of *him*!"

Fool.

Idiot.

Loudmouth.

"Who?" Mom asked.

I wasn't going to say it.

But Heather knew. *All* my friends knew now.
Mom was bound to find out sooner or later.
I took a breath. "Dad," I mumbled.

"You were with Dad?"

"No. See, I thought I saw Dad. On the platform."

Mom stopped short. "You mean — like a
homeless person, living on the tracks? *Oh,
David, why didn't you tell me?"*

"No. No. It wasn't him, Mom. It wasn't any-
body. It was a hallucination."

Mom's whole body seemed to cave in.
"David Moore, are you making this up?"

"No!"

"Are you just *pretending* you thought you
saw Dad? Like that would make me forgive
you for walking onto that platform? Like,
'The stress made me do it, Mom'?"

"Forget it — "

"Do not play with me, David. I have not

slept for months. I jump when the phone rings. I feel as if my insides have been pulled out and dragged across the country. And as much as I love you and try to understand how you're feeling, I will not let you use your father as an excuse to behave like a monster!"

Mom's words were furious, but her eyes told a different story. They were saying, *Tell me it's true.* Behind the fear and confusion and numbness was hope, like the gray light before a sunrise.

I couldn't speak. That hope was doing something to me. Pulling me inside her. For a moment, I felt the shock of Dad's death all over again. Through her eyes.

Pictures flashed in my mind — the old pictures in our hallway. Dad as a skinny young guy with a ponytail and a muscle shirt. Pointing to his crew cut in mock horror after he joined the force. Kissing Mom at their wedding. All images of Dad before I knew him. A stranger, really.

My own mental picture of Dad was so different. He was older, grayer, and heavier. *That* was the dad I had lost.

In a way, though, Mom had lost *all* those men on the wall. Every single one.

I realized she was feeling pain I could never know.

And now she was looking to me for an answer. For hope.

Well, I knew something about hope now. It transforms you. It's like a mirage in the desert. You see it where it doesn't exist. On a TV show. In the blank expression of a detective.

On a rotting subrail platform.

And just like a mirage, it lets you down. Hard.

I couldn't give that hope to Mom. It wasn't fair.

If I was cracking up, I didn't need to drag her down with me.

"It's stupid, Mom," I said, looking away. "Just . . . like a hallucination or something. I haven't been feeling right lately. That's all . . ."

My voice trailed off. For a long time, Mom didn't reply.

Then I felt her arm around my shoulders.

"David," she said gently, "I think we both need a vacation."

What I needed first, however, was a shower. Which I took right away when we arrived home.

Afterward I headed straight to my room. I carefully closed the door, then dumped onto my desk the contents of my pocket — a Yumm-E wrapper, subrail tokens, keys, two rubber bands, a jumbo paper clip . . .

The sky-blue card was tucked into a folded-up homework assignment.

My stomach started to flutter.

Hope.

No.

Get rid of it. Don't even look.

I ran to the bathroom and lifted the toilet seat.

With one hand I grabbed the flusher. With the other hand I held the card over the bowl.

And I read the words.

This was not part of the plan.

In order to get closer,
you sometimes must fall behind.

9

THE SKY'S THE LIMIT

Environmental Consultants

☆ Miles Ruckman ☆

Administrative Assistant

9972-7660

My heart stopped pounding.

The name didn't ring any bells. Neither did the company.

Just a guy. A normal guy.

A guy whose business card had floated onto the subrail platform yesterday.

I pulled the card away from the toilet. What if Miles Ruckman needed it? Maybe it was his last one.

Call him.

I had to. I had to hear his voice and know he was alive in Franklin City. Not off in some phantom world.

I snuck into Mom's bedroom and picked up the voicephone.

"David?" she called out from the kitchen. "Any lunch requests? I'm going to the food shop!"

"Uh . . . hot dogs?" I called out. "Ice cream? Chocolate-stripe cookies?"

Mom chuckled. "Okay, well, stick around while I'm gone, okay?"

"Sure."

I waited until I heard the front door close. The ding of the elevator bell.

Alone.

I held up the business card and reached for the voicephone.

BLEEEEEEP!

I nearly hit the ceiling.

I grabbed the receiver. *"Hello?"*

"What's wrong?"

Heather. It figured.

"Nothing's wrong! What do you want?"

"What's it say? The card?"

"Why should I tell you?"

"If it weren't for me, you wouldn't have gotten it."

"If it weren't for you, I wouldn't have been *arrested*!"

"True. But you're only thirteen. They just scared you and slapped you on the wrist, right?"

"How do you know?"

"I watch TV. So, what does the card say?"

I exhaled. No use fighting a force of nature. "Some guy's name. I was about to call him before you interrupted."

"Was it the guy who disappeared?"

"No one *disappeared*, Heather."

"Oh, yeah, right, it was a hallucination. I forgot. So why are you calling him?"

"To tell him he lost his card, okay?"

"I'll be right over."

Click.

I waited for the buzz tone. Then I carefully tapped out the number printed on the card.

"This is The Sky's the Limit," came a recorded voice. "Our regular business hours are — "

Ding-dong-ding-dong-ding-dong-ding-dong!

I slammed down the receiver, ran to the front door, and opened it.

"That was fast," I said.

"Is this it?" Heather blurted out, grabbing the card from my hand as she barged inside. "Let's call."

"I just did. The company's closed. We can't talk to him until after the weekend, I guess."

"Duh." Heather went straight to the kitchen, took a residential directory off the shelf, and leafed through it furiously. "Here it is! 'Ruckman, Miles . . . 9766-1848.' "

Sometimes I can't stand smart people.

I called the number.

But I reached another recorded voice, stiff and dull-sounding: "This is Miles Ruckman. I'm unable to answer your call right now, but if you'd like to leave — "

"*Auuuugh.*" I hung up again. "He's not home, either."

"That proves it!" Heather exclaimed. "He *did* vanish."

"He could be anywhere. Out shopping. In the bathroom."

"Okay, we'll wait and call again." Heather was fiddling impatiently with the business card now, turning it around. "Hey, what's this?"

She held the back of the card toward me. On it was a scribbled message:

GRN LINE
BETW BOOKR AND DRFIELD
HI EV.BODY WISH U WERE HERE
— A PERSSON

"Great speller," I commented.

"Yyyyyyes!" Heather leaped up and began dancing. "Between Booker and Deerfield! That's where the Granite Street station is. *Right here in his own handwriting!*"

"He wrote down the location. Big deal. Heather, lots of people like to gawk at the station."

"And then they just toss their business cards out the door?" Heather stuffed the card in her shirt pocket and glanced at the directory again. "He lives at 37 Bond Street. We can ring his buzzer. If he's not there, we can stay until he arrives. *If* he arrives. Are you with me?"

"You're crazy. That's . . . that's stalking!"

Heather started for the door. "I'll go. I'll let you know what happens."

"Wait!" I said.

Heather turned around.

"There's a cool vintage comic book store on Bond Street," I mumbled. "Maybe I'll go down there with you."

We took the subrail. The phantom station was as empty and dark as usual.

Thirty-seven Bond was a rundown apartment building, close to the river. A rusted fire escape zigzagged down the front of it, and a few garbage cans stood empty on the sidewalk.

Near the front door was a list of names and apartment numbers, each next to its own black push button — just like my building, where you ring a buzzer to someone's apartment and that person buzzes you inside.

Right away we spotted M. RUCKMAN 3E.

Heather pressed his buzzer, then raised an eyebrow. "Comic book store, huh?" she said slyly.

"Uh, well, I'll just see if he answers," I said. "Then I'll go."

We waited a few moments, then Heather pressed again.

"No one home," I said.

"Guess I'll have to go inside and wait by his apartment door." Heather began pressing all the buttons on the board.

"Hey!" I protested. "What are you — ?"

BZZZZZZZ!

Heather pushed the door and it swung open.

"See? If you buzz them all, someone's bound to let you in," she said. "Coming?"

I followed Heather into a dark hallway with a worn-out tile floor. The air was stuffy and smelled of fried food. At the end of the hallway, we climbed a dark, lopsided stairway, passing gray windows that were permanently shut by years of caked paint.

Apartment 3E was at the end of a long, narrow hallway. At the other end, the doors to apartments 3A and 3B faced each other in a small alcove. We could hide there, unseen by Miles Ruckman when he returned.

"What if he's gone for the whole day?" I whispered. "Or the weekend?"

Heather shrugged. "We come back another time."

"How long do we stay?"

"Until we get bored."

I sighed. "I don't know *why* I agreed to do this — "

"Then go to the comic book store!"

Click.

We both shut up.

The noise came from down the hall. A doorknob.

Heather and I peeked around the alcove wall.

A door was opening. The door to apartment 3E.

The breath caught in my throat. Heather's eyes were bulging.

A stoop-shouldered figure pushed out into the hallway, wearing a long, tattered overcoat.

I caught a glimpse of the person's face as

he turned, before I ducked back into the alcove.

"Oh my God," I said under my breath.

"Isn't that — ?" Heather whispered.

I nodded. "Anders."

Why now?

Why not?

10

"What's *he* doing there?" Heather hissed.

"You're asking me?" I hissed back.

"Did he see us?"

"Sssshhh!"

Shhhhip . . . shhhip . . . shhhip . . .

Anders's shoes were scraping the linoleum floor. Coming closer.

My breathing stopped. Heather shrank deeper into the shadows.

Shhhhip.

Anders was just outside the alcove now.

Inches away. I could hear him muttering to himself. Indistinct words. Growls.

Then . . . *Thump. Thump. Thump. Thump.* He was going downstairs.

I thought my lungs would explode. I let out a whoosh of breath.

Neither Heather nor I moved until we heard the front door of the apartment building open and shut.

"He's a burglar!" Heather said.

I shook my head. "It's broad daylight. Maybe he has a key. Maybe he's a friend of Miles Ruckman."

"A friend of Miles Ruckman, a friend of your dad . . . could there *possibly* be a connection?"

"Don't start, Heather," I said, heading out of the alcove. "Just don't start."

"You have to admit, it's strange. Don't deny it!"

I began walking downstairs. I was in no mood for Heather's crazy theories. I was not going to listen.

But I was not going to deny it, either. Something awfully weird was going on.

* * *

"I'm home!" I shouted as I entered our apartment.

The door slammed behind me. I flung my backpack into the living room.

I was still thinking about Anders, so I almost didn't notice the change in the front hallway.

The wall was empty. All the photos were gone, leaving faded rectangles.

"Where were you?" Mom stormed in from her bedroom. "I thought I told you — "

"Heather called. She needed help with . . . something. You know how she is. So. What happened to all the pictures?"

Mom nodded grudgingly toward her bedroom. Her anger seemed to melt away as we walked inside.

All the photos were stacked on her bed, along with piles of notebooks, photo albums, and papers. I turned to Mom and she smiled at me sadly. I could see she'd been crying.

In the corner of the room stood Dad's desk, its drawers open and empty. All that was left on top was his old world globe.

"What are you doing with Dad's stuff?" I asked.

"I thought it was time to change things," Mom replied. "Freshen up the house. Paint the walls. Clean out Dad's desk — you know, so you can use it while he's . . . gone."

Mom's voice caught. She began busily shuffling papers around.

I sat at the edge of the crowded bed. It was a weird feeling — as if Dad were in the room, his spirit spread out on the bedcover. I opened a photo album marked with the year of my birth. On the first page was a picture of Dad leaning over a white bassinet. He had a lot of hair and a trim beard. His eyes were narrow and puffy, as if he hadn't slept, but his smile could have lit up the entire city.

Mom glanced at it. "You were two weeks old. Dad woke up every time you made the slightest sound. He cared so much about you."

My eyes started to water. Partly because of the photo. But that wasn't the only reason.

Mom had said "cared." Past tense.

She was finally forcing herself to face the truth. Putting away reminders for good.

I picked up a copy of my third-grade report card. A program from my summer camp play.

A button I'd bought Dad at a fair that said MY SON IS CRAZY ABOUT ME!

Mom held up a small dog-eared spiral notebook. "Did you know your dad used to keep journals, just like you do?"

"No," I replied. But it didn't surprise me. Dad loved to write. For a while he even had a regular column for the Franklin City Public Guardian newsletter.

"He stopped when you were in second grade or so. Things got too busy. Listen to this." Mom held up the book and began reading aloud: " 'Picked up D from preschool today. Two of his friends ran to parents, screaming, "I love you *this* much," holding arms wide, like a contest. D started crying. He said, "My arms aren't big enough to do that, Daddy. 'Cause I love you . . ." ' "

" ' . . . from the tips of my toes to the top of the universe,' " I continued. "I remember."

" 'Wow!' " Mom's voice trembled as she continued reading. " 'This is what I call happiness.' " She stopped and put down the notebook. "Excuse me, David."

She left quickly. Soon I could hear her sniffling behind the closed bathroom door.

As I blinked tears from my own eyes, I noticed five or six other journals piled on the bed. Dad had scrawled a beginning and end date on each. I looked for old ones, from when he was a kid. My age, maybe. But the earliest was written the year before Mom and Dad married.

I was tempted to open one, but I couldn't. Reading Dad's journals seemed wrong. Like an invasion of his privacy.

In fact, this whole project was making me nervous. I stood up to go back to my room. As I passed Dad's desk, I gave the globe a spin.

It wobbled jerkily on its base, then plopped onto its side and began rolling. I grabbed it before it reached the edge of the desk.

When I was a kid, Dad never liked me to play with his globe. Now I knew why. What a lousy design.

As I lifted it upright, I could feel something thump lightly inside.

That was when I noticed the two small fingerholds, one on either side of the equator. And the hinge in the curved metal support that connected the globe's axis to its base.

I looked over toward the bathroom. The

door was shut and I could hear the water running.

I put my fingers into the holds and pulled. The globe opened into two halves.

Inside was another journal.

I took it out and looked at the cover.

It had only one date written on it. A beginning date, about two years ago. After that date was a hyphen, then nothing.

As if Dad hadn't finished it.

I flipped to the last page. On the top, a date had been scribbled.

The day before Dad disappeared.

Underneath it was a page filled with Dad's handwriting.

Forget privacy.

I sat down to read.

He is hurting.

That, I'm afraid, is beyond our control.

11

*Hard 2 hold pen now. Mine is
Mind is gong going. T thinks Im crazy
Cannot pos make her understand.*

T stood for Mom's name, Taylor.

Awful memories flooded in. Mom and Dad shouting in the kitchen. His slurred words. Her sobs. Loud. So loud I had to bury my head under my pillow.

You're drunk! Mom would shout. But he

wasn't. His disease — whatever it was — was beginning.

Still, Dad's entry didn't make sense. By the time he wrote it, Mom did understand. She *knew* he was sick.

Cant ~~copsens copseti~~ think. Dont have much longer. Can feel it. Have 2 go home - Dont want 2. Told T. ~~Shes~~ not ready 2 hear it.

Home?
That was the last word Dad had said to Mom. She had asked, *Where are you going at this hour?* and he had answered, *Home.*
But what did it mean? He *was* home.
Unless . . .
Another home. Another life.
A family somewhere else.
Impossible.
Ridiculous.
But my mind was sifting back through the years. Back to all the business trips Dad used to take. He'd be gone for days, on assignment — "helping the pugs," he said.

Was he lying all that time?

Lying so he could visit them?

I'd heard of cases like this. But *Dad*?

Told T, he'd written.

So Mom knew about it. Mom knew about his secret life. And she was covering it up.

No. I refused to believe this.

I flipped back a few pages. There had to be an explanation.

The click of the bathroom door caught me off guard.

I slammed the globe shut. Quickly I stuffed the journal into my rear pants pocket, letting my loose T-shirt hang over it.

"Sorry, David." Mom walked into the room, dabbing her eyes. "When I read passages like that I feel so guilty. Sometimes I forget what a good guy your dad was."

"Was he?" *Easy, David.*

Mom gave me a funny look. "Yes, of course, David . . ."

"I mean, I was just thinking about when you and Dad used to argue . . . he said some weird stuff, didn't he?"

"He was very ill," Mom said with a sigh.

"You must understand it wasn't his fault."

"Didn't he say something about . . . going *home*?"

Mom sat down on the bed, her face clouding over. "Yes, he did. I'd hoped you hadn't heard that . . ."

"Where, Mom? Where's his other home?"

"It's — " Mom cut herself off and choked back a sob. "David, promise me it's not going to happen to you, too."

"Promise *what's* not going to happen?"

Mom collected herself. Taking a deep breath, she looked me straight in the eye. "Remember how upset I was this morning at the FCSS headquarters? Well, it wasn't only about what you did. It was also about what you saw."

"I *told* you that was just a daydream — "

"That's where home was, David."

Mom let the words hang in the air. They began dropping into my crazy thoughts like embers on dry brush.

"The Granite Street station," Mom continued. "That's where Dad said his home was."

One at a time.

Her, too?

12

"Ask me if I'm surprised. No, I'm not." Heather was practically dancing on her carpet. "I've been telling you all along — your dad's in the station, and he's looking for you."

"Heather, I think it might have all been a lie — Dad's sickness, his behavior . . ." I showed her his final journal, which I'd brought with me. "I've been reading these diaries. I think he was leading a double life. Like, another wife and kids."

Heather gave me a wary look. "That's crazy."

"Any crazier than what *you* believe? Think about it. No doctor could diagnose the disease. He'd wander off for days at a time — "

"Your dad didn't lie — "

"He was a case solver. He specialized in mysteries. He knew how people kept secrets and got away with them. And he was full of his own secrets. Like his past."

"He was an orphan. He didn't like to talk about it. You always told me that."

"And I never questioned it. Doesn't it seem weird that he wrote in these journals *every day* but not before he met my mom?"

Heather took the journal and began leafing through it. "This doesn't make sense . . . 'D' this, 'T' that . . ."

I looked over her shoulder. As she flipped through, my eyes caught something familiar.

I pressed my palm to the page, holding the journal open. And I read:

A P wont go w me. Has four tokens. tho. Says better to shuffle off mortal coil here than face injustice home. Typical.

" 'Home,' " I said. "There it is again."

"Who's this AP?" Heather asked. "And what's 'shuffle off mortal coil' mean?"

"Don't you know? You're the genius."

Heather shrugged. "Sounds like language from some other century. Your dad never said stuff like that."

"True. I guess AP did, though."

AP.

It hit me.

I picked up Heather's voicephone. "Heather, you *are* a genius."

"Who are you calling?" Heather asked.

I tapped out my home number.

"Hello?" came Mom's voice.

"Mom, what's Anders's last name?"

"Pearson," I heard her say. "Why?"

Heather was right next to me now. I turned to face her. "Did you say *Pearson*, Mom? *Anders Pearson?*"

Heather looked blank for a moment, then beamed.

"Yes," Mom said. "Why?"

"Ask her how he spells it!" Heather hissed.

I covered the receiver. *"Why?"*

"David, what's going on?" Mom's voice asked.

"Um, Mom, how do you spell that? P-E-A-R —?"

Heather grabbed the receiver and put her own ear close to mine.

"No, David," Mom said. "It's *P-E-R-S-S-O-N.*"

I thought Heather was going to faint.

A. PERSSON.

He's smart.

That's why we need him.

13

GRN LiNE
BETW BOOKR AND DRFiELD
Hi EV. BODY WiSH U WERE HERE
— A PERSSON

I must have read the back of Miles Ruckman's business card a dozen times as we left Heather's apartment and raced down the stairwell.

"Anders was sending a message to the other world," Heather said over her shoulder. "The message was 'Hi everybody. Wish you were here.' And Ruckman was supposed to deliver it."

"But he dropped the card," I replied.

"Right! So you believe me?"

"Maybe. I don't know."

We pushed through the door to the eighth floor.

Anders lived in 8B. I pressed the doorbell.

"Rrraoogllf," crackled a voice from inside.

"Mr. Persson?" I shouted. "It's David Moore. Alan's son?"

The door opened a crack and a bloodshot eye peered out. "Yeah?" Anders said.

"Did you lose this?" I handed him the business card.

He looked at it briefly. "Nope."

The door began to shut, but I stuck my foot in the opening.

"What about the other side?" Heather said.

I turned the card over and pointed to the handwritten message. "You wrote this, didn't you?"

"So?" Anders growled.

"Miles Ruckman dropped it," Heather said.

"What did the message mean? 'Hi everybody, wish you were here'? Where was he taking it?"

"To his office," Anders replied. "Now, go away."

"But he's gone, isn't he?" Heather asked. "And you've been to his empty apartment."

"I will call the guardians!" Anders cried out.

"Did he shuffle off his mortal coil?" Heather blurted out. "Like you wanted David's dad to do?"

Anders let his door slowly open. A thick, musty smell wafted out of the apartment, like old socks and moldy potatoes. "Shakespeare," he muttered. "How do you know — ?"

Heather poked me in the ribs. "Tell him where you found the card, David."

"In the Granite Street station," I said. "On the platform."

"What were you doing there?" Anders asked.

"That was where Miles Ruckman dropped it," Heather replied.

"A few days ago, while I was riding the train home, it stopped there," I explained.

"The platform was full. Clean and all lit up. With posters on the wall. Miles Ruckman was in the car. But when the door opened, he walked out. He was holding the card, as if he wanted to give it to someone. Then the door closed and the train took off. And . . . and I saw my dad."

Anders's restless eyes were now steady and bright. "You saw your dad. And on your way to him you picked up Ruckman's card."

"No. I stayed on the train. I picked up the card on another trip."

"Another trip . . ." Anders looked from me to Heather.

Heather was grinning with triumph. "So? Talk to us?"

Anders let out a giggle. Then, in a sudden burst, it became a loud, wild cackle. "You must think I'm awfully stupid."

With that, he slammed the door shut.

Good.

14

My arm whipped into the swiftly closing crack.

"*Go away!*" Anders cried. "*I don't believe you!*"

"Open it!" I yelled in pain.

"*Let go!*" Heather screamed, ramming her shoulder into the door.

It swung open.

Anders was backing into the room. "You're wired for sound, aren't you?" he asked. "You're taping me. You're going to play it for the U.S. marshals!"

Heather shot me a confused glance. "We don't know what you're talking about, Anders," she replied.

I heard the click of a lock down the hall. A neighbor's opening door.

We stepped into Anders's apartment. The door swung shut.

Anders had backed in as far as he could go. His home was one small room. Everywhere I looked — the floor, the furniture, the windowsills — lay piles of old clothing, half-empty containers of food, open books, yellowing newspapers. The windows were shut tight and the smell was overpowering.

Heather grimaced. "Yuck."

"You're trespassing!" Anders shouted. "I'll call the pugs."

"Anders," I said, "we just want to ask you questions —"

"Is that what they told you to say?" Anders barked a desperate laugh. "What a cliché. Like an old World War Two movie. Did they show those to you for training? In between European literature lessons? What else, huh? Spy novels? Rich culture, ain't it?"

He was gone. Out of his mind. His words made no sense.

"Let's go, Heather," I said.

Anders had pressed himself against a dirty wall, covered with old strips of tape that no longer held anything. "Your dad's one of them now, isn't he? That's why he wanted me to cross over. And now he went and hired you two. Maybe Ruckman, too."

"Hired?" Heather repeated.

"He's crazy," I whispered. *"Come on!"*

"It's an act," Heather replied.

"Or maybe you want to throw me into an asylum," Anders continued. "Is that it?"

"A what?" I asked.

"Asylum, loony bin, nuthouse — " Anders burst out laughing. "Of course, you don't know the idiom! *One Flew Over the Cuckoo's Nest.* Rings no bells, eh?"

"Uh . . . no," Heather said calmly. "Mr. Persson, look, we're not . . . whatever you think we are. David has seen into another dimension, that's all. It happens. The problem is, he can't see it anymore, but he wants to, because his dad is trying to speak to him."

"Tell them they'll have to take me back dead. Give them back their money. It's worthless here anyway." Anders stumbled across the room and opened a dresser drawer. Reaching behind a mass of wrinkled underwear, he pulled out a stack of bills and held them out to me.

They were a funny shade of green, like play money.

Out of curiosity, I took one bill and examined it. The design was intricate, but I didn't recognize the portrait in the center.

"Maybe I can help, Mr. Persson," Heather pleaded. "I want to see this other world. I've tried, but I can't. What do I have to do? I mean, do you technically need a relative who lives there, like David has? Or did David just happen to see it at just the right alignment of time and space or something — you know, like a parallel world that only happens, like, once every hundred years, and now it's too late?"

She was as crazy as he was.

"Heather, let's get out of here!"

"Do you need passage — is that what this is all about?" Anders pulled three small, odd-looking coins from his drawer and held them out to Heather. "Here. If I give you these, will you go?"

Heather took one and held it up to the light. " 'Good for one fare,' " she read aloud. "These are some kind of subrail tokens." She looked curiously at Anders.

"Yes," Anders said with a wild smile. "And they'll work. If you're meant to use them."

"How do you know if you're meant to use them?" Heather asked.

"If they work!" Anders howled with laughter.

Looking at Heather, I raised an impatient eyebrow. "Now?"

"Oh! Oh!" Anders was gasping to control his hilarity. " 'What shall it profit a man, if he shall gain the whole world, and lose his own soul?' "

Heather nodded. "Now."

I pocketed the tokens and the money, and we both left, letting the door slam behind us.

Anders's hysterical howls followed us down the hallway.

We never thought of the tokens.

We're not perfect.

15

Feet. Pounding the pavement.
Voices. Battling inside my head.
He's insane.
But he was Dad's friend.
*A filbert who lives in filth, spouts nonsense,
and collects play money.*
But he knew the place Dad called "home."
And we were taking him seriously. Running to the subrail station like little kids. To test what he'd said. About the tokens. About the other world.
It was worth a try.

No.

"Heather, why are we doing this?" I called out.

Heather was already a half block ahead of me, bounding down the subrail stairs. "Hurry!"

I followed her. Against my better judgment. Against logic. Against every instinct. Knowing I'd face nothing but frustration.

But I couldn't help it. Hope, that dormant little germ, was waking inside of me. Infecting me.

I'd forgotten what hope felt like.

If Anders is right, the pieces of the mystery fit.

I could not get that idea out of my mind. Because if you thought about it, Anders's wacko story explained Dad's journal entry.

"AP" was wanted for a crime. That would account for all the money — Anders stole it and somehow slipped into our world. And when I said I'd "seen" Dad, Anders freaked out. He thought I'd crossed to the other world, too — and met some pugs there, who sent me back with a secret tape recorder to help catch him . . .

Moore, you have lost it. Dad was insane himself when he wrote that stuff. The journal was nonsense!

Dad lived in this world. *This* world was his home.

And why even *think* of trusting Anders? Who was he, anyway? For all we knew, he could have been a serial killer. Maybe he was luring us to the Granite Street station. Maybe he kept his victims there. Under the platform.

Maybe Dad was one victim. Then Miles Ruckman. Now us.

Heather was at the rotary gates now, looking around for me as people bustled by her. *"Where are the tokens?"* she pleaded.

"Heather, I have a problem with this," I said. "I mean, what if this whole thing was made up? What if Anders — "

"Just give one to me!" Heather demanded. "Your problem, David, is that you *doubt* too much!"

I dug my hand into my pocket and pulled out one of Anders's tokens.

Totally the wrong size. I knew it. Too small and too light.

I dropped it into the slot.

It rattled downward. I quickly pushed the metal rotary gate.

It didn't budge.

With a feeble clink, the token landed in the coin return slot.

Rejected.

Can we get him back?

We still have a few tricks.

16

I am dreaming, and in my dream I am riding the Green Line. Calmly. After that experience with Heather at the rotary gate today, I am much wiser. Now I know that my vision of Dad was just that. A vision. It is perfectly, rationally explainable.

It was caused by power of suggestion. Months ago, I must have heard Dad talk about the station. I must have heard him tell Mom about his imaginary "home." I wasn't conscious of hearing it, but the words stayed in my mind. And months later, after Dad was gone and I was under stress, the image appeared to me. As for the blue business card, it had probably been lying on the platform for ages. Crazy Anders must have thrown it there. I probably saw it many times without taking notice — and it worked its way into my fantasy, too.

Simple.

I will definitely major in psychology in college.

So in my dream, as I'm reading my newspaper, I don't even look up when the Granite Street station approaches.

Not even as the train begins to slow down.

Only when the lights go out do I peek out the window.

And there's Dad. Waiting outside the door. Smiling. Looking totally healthy.

The door slides open. Nobody is moving or noticing, just as before.

"Come," Dad is saying. "Don't doubt."

I try to get up. But I can't. My arms and legs are frozen.

I open my mouth to speak, but all that comes out is a moan.

Now Dad is beginning to fade. "I will come for you," he says.

"D — D —" Nothing. My mouth is locked.

"Alan . . . ALAN!" It's Mom's voice. She's in the train, too! I turn to her. I want her to stop Dad from disappearing. I try to plead with her, but —

"ALAAAAAAAN!"

My eyes opened. It *was* Mom's voice. Calling for Dad. From her bedroom.

I sprang out of bed. My dream was still with me.

I shook all over as I tiptoed closer to Mom's room.

Her door was open a crack.

"Stay . . . there!" Mom was crying in a sleep-slurred voice. "Don't fade, Alan! Let me come for *you!*"

It won't work if we force it.
The sight will drive him crazy.

Or it will set him free.

17

"**D**o you have *any* idea what time it is, David?" came Heather's groggy voice through the receiver.

"Sorry, but I had to call you," I whispered. "I want to try again."

"*What?* David, are you, like, talking in your sleep? Because if that's the reason you interrupted my beauty rest — "

"The phantom station, Heather! I don't doubt it anymore. Mom and I were having the same dream. Dad is calling to us. She's still sleeping, but I can't. I have to go to the station. Meet me in the lobby?"

"Do you know what's out on the street in Franklin City at this hour?"

"Fifteen minutes?"

"You got it."

I was there in twelve. Heather was already there, waiting.

We sprinted outside. The city streets were eerily quiet. Our breath made wispy puffs in the air as our footsteps echoed hollowly on the sidewalk.

Once again we bounded down the station steps. This time the place was deserted, except for a sleeping clerk in the fare booth.

Heather was heading for the rotary gate.

"Wait," I said.

I took two of Anders's tokens out of my pocket. I gave one to Heather. I'd made sure to leave the third one at home. In plain sight on Mom's dresser.

Heather and I faced each other across a gate. I inserted my token into the slot. As it dropped, I pushed.

This time, it worked.

I thought Heather's jaw would hit the ground.

She dropped her token in and followed me through.

"Pinch?" Heather said, holding out her arm.

I did. And she pinched my arm.

We were real.

We were meant to do this. Just as Anders had said.

The train was coming. Clattering closer.

We walked to the edge of the platform.

With a roar made even louder than usual by the empty station, the train pulled in.

We entered. As the door closed behind us, we did not bother to sit.

The train began to move. It picked up speed as it hurtled into the tunnel.

In a moment, it began to slow. Heather squeezed my hand.

Blackness.

A screech of brakes. We were stopping.

And then, the light.

Bright.

Searing.

In my face.

I had to shield my eyes.

"I can't see!" I shouted.

No answer.

Pain. Hot, ripping pain. "This isn't like the last time," I cried out. "Something's wrong."

Heather wasn't moving. She was still facing the door, holding my hand firmly.

The train was now still.

And I heard the whoosh of the opening door.

Now.

18

I tried to open my eyes to the light.

And I began to shake.

Heather's face was silhouetted. Almost translucent. And she was staring straight ahead.

"Heather, close your eyes!" I cried.

Smiling. I could now see she was smiling.

And I could see something else, too. A movement, reflected in her deep brown irises.

It was a figure, growing larger.

I turned toward it, but my lids automatically shut.

Run.

My feet were ready. My body was poised.

But I stood there.

And soon my shaking stopped.

I drew slow, deep breaths. And with each one the pain lessened, a little at a time, then more and more until I felt as if I were blowing it away in big gusts.

When it was gone, when my eyes no longer ached, I opened them.

The brightness still remained. But it didn't hurt. It was only light now. Light without heat. Without hurt.

And I saw the figure I'd spotted in Heather's eyes. Stepping through the light, his arms reaching out to me.

"Dad?"

His smile put the surrounding brightness to shame. His eyes were slits, as if he'd been sleeping. But he looked healthy. Healthy, like he used to be.

"This is a heck of an hour to do this," Dad said.

Go. It's safe.

I leaped at him. I felt as if ten years had

stripped away and I was three again, ecstatic that Dad had come home from work.

I'd forgotten how that felt.

This was better. Much better.

I heard the whoosh of the train door again. I turned around.

Heather was inside, looking at us through the glass. Tears were streaming down her cheeks.

"Heather!" I cried out. "What are you doing?"

She waved, smiling, as the train pulled away.

"It's all right," Dad said. "She knows she doesn't belong here. You do."

The dresser. The token on Mom's dresser.

"TELL MY MOM — " I yelled to Heather.

But it was useless. The train's noise swallowed my words.

Dad put a hand on my shoulder, and I turned toward him again.

This time I took a longer look at his face.

Clean-shaven. Bright-eyed. Sane.

"Dad, are you — okay now?" I began.

Dad nodded. "They can treat my disease

here. Unfortunately, we weren't built to cross over, David. At least not for long periods of time. I learned that the hard way. Our bodies react. I had to come home."

"So you — you're *from* this . . . this world? And Anders — "

"He's from here, too. He was a brilliant guy, a scholar. No one suspected he was a thief, too."

"Except you."

"He knew about the subway station, David — or subrail, as you call it. We crossed over together while I was chasing him. Then, once we were on the other side, what could I do? Arrest him?"

"So you just stayed?"

"I didn't mean to. I figured I'd wait Anders out, until he got homesick or something, then take him back in handcuffs. But I kind of liked being a new person in a new place. And Anders and I became buddies. Odd how that happens. We moved into Wiggins Street . . . and then I met your mom."

"And had me."

"And never regretted a minute of it," Dad said.

"So . . . your childhood . . . your parents . . ."

"I lied to you. I'm sorry. It wasn't a very convincing story, I know. But it's the first one I thought of, and I had to stick to it. And you do have grandparents. I'll introduce you, when the time is right."

"So . . . you just left them . . . and then you left us."

Dad smiled sadly. "Sometimes you have to lose a world to gain your soul."

"I've heard something like that." I thought back. "Anders said it!"

Dad's smile vanished. "Actually, it's from the New Testament. Anders often quoted from it — and from Shakespeare and a thousand others. The sickness hit poor Anders a lot earlier than it did me. He didn't want to return, though, not with a bounty on his head. But when *I* started to lose it, I knew I had to come back. I tried to tell Mom, but she wasn't ready to hear."

"I left a token on her dresser," I blurted out. "But Heather doesn't know — "

"You did the right thing, David. We've been working on Mom, too, you know."

"We?"

"I mean, *I*. Between the two of us, we'll get her here."

"So . . . this is it? We'll all be living . . . here?"

"We'll just have to figure that one out, won't we?" Dad sighed and put his arm around my shoulders.

As we walked away from the track, I was noticing the station around me. The gray cement floors. The tiled walls. The strange ads.

A new world.

"It's not bad here," Dad said confidently. "You may like it."

"What about school? Am I going to have to learn about all that stuff Anders talked about? What's World War Two?"

"Where you come from is a good place, David," Dad said with a laugh, "but I think ours is more interesting."

"They sure have more signs in the subrails here." I pointed to one I'd noticed before. "Why does that say 'us open'?"

"That's U.S.," Dad replied. "It stands for United States — the name of your new country. The U.S. Open is a sports event. Tennis."

" 'New York City' . . . 'Bronx' . . . weird names."

"To be honest, those places don't look much different than Franklin City. I mean, they do occupy the same space, sort of."

"What do you call the planet?"

"Earth."

I shivered. So much was going to be different. "You've got to be kidding. Sounds like a burp noise."

Dad burst out laughing. "Believe me, David, you get used to it."

He sounded so sure.

I wasn't.

I had a feeling I hadn't even begun to understand what had happened to me.

Congratulations.

Congratulate *him*.

In due time.

WATCHERS
Case File: 3583

Name: David Moore

Age: 13

First contact: 33.35.67

Acceptance: YES

ABOUT THE AUTHOR

Peter Lerangis lives in New York City, five blocks from the real subway station that inspired this book. He has written two popular thrillers, *The Yearbook* and *Drivers Dead*, as well as *It Came from the Cafeteria*, *Attack of the Killer Potatoes*, *Spring Fever*, and *Spring Break*.

Look for the next
WATCHERS
REWIND

Adam felt cold. Cold and alone.

Darkness had swallowed the woods. His path was vanishing fast.

"Guys?"

The word died in the air, swept away by a shriek of north wind. Above him, branches waved wildly in the moonlight, clattering like old, brittle bones.

This was a stupid idea, Sarno.

He shouldn't have agreed to play laser tag. Especially here. Especially at this time of year, when the reminders were so strong.

He tried not to think of what had happened. It was four years ago. He had to get over it. He couldn't avoid the lake his whole life.

Thump.

Adam's heart nearly stopped.

"Ripley?" he called out. "Lianna?"

No answer.

Maybe they were hiding from him. Listening to his voice. Laughing at how it sounded. Timid. Scared. So very *Adam.*

(*Adam is a wimp . . .*)

Or maybe they'd left already. The lovebirds running off, not telling anyone.

Not Lianna. She'd never do that to me.

But Ripley would.

Okay, fine.

I am not afraid.

I know these woods.

I am ten blocks from home.

He slung his laser gun over his shoulder. To his right, the woods disappeared into blackness. To his left, the moon peeked through the trees, dimly lighting a path toward the lake. He could follow the trail along the bank to the big clearing, where his bike was.

Stay away from the lake.

Adam ignored the thought. He was older now. Too old to be afraid.

It was only a memory.

Memories couldn't hurt you.

As he trudged to the lake, his heart began to race.

The warning signs were legible even in the faint moonlight: DANGER! THIN ICE! DO NOT ENTER UNDER PENALTY OF LAW!

Adam glanced beyond the signs. The lake looked remote. Unfriendly.

The last time he was on the lake the signs didn't exist. You could sneak onto the ice and no one bothered you.

But the last time was four years ago. A January afternoon.

He did sneak onto the ice that day. To practice hockey.

Don't think about this now. Turn away.

But Adam's eyes fixed on a distant spot on the snow-dusted ice. In line with a clump of pine trees at the opposite bank.

That was where it had happened.

Lianna had been there. She had come along with

Don't.

With Edgar.

Edgar didn't want to practice. I forced him.

They were ten. The hockey net was heavy, and no one was helping Adam set it up. Edgar was skating around, teasing Adam (*showing off for Lianna*), challenging him to take away the puck, being a total jerk, and (*I wanted to kill him*) that was it, wasn't it, that was the reason for the fight (*it's not my fault*), and when Edgar was fished out of the hole, he had a big bump on his head (*because it hit the ice*), but Adam couldn't remember because he'd fallen in, too, and blacked out, and if it weren't for Lianna he would have died himself, which would have made more sense, because what did poor Edgar do to deserve what he got, a deadly blow to the head from his supposed best friend?

It's not my fault.

And the next thing Adam remembered, he was in the hospital, screaming (*Edgar! Edgar!*), while the doctors scratched their chins and told him it wasn't his fault (*they didn't see it, only Lianna did*) and from then on, everything was different, he couldn't concentrate, and the kids at school steered clear of him — but the rumors got back (*Adam killed Edgar, whacked him in the head, pushed him into a hole in the ice and tried to run away*), the rumors he ignored even though *they were true, weren't they?*

Stop.

He began to run. Away from the lake. Blindly. His laser pack and coat snagged on brambles, but he didn't care. He had to get away. He had to go home.

But where's Edgar? I can't leave without Edgar.

The thoughts were following him. Taunting him.

Edgar is dead.

Dead. Dead. Dead.

"Help!"

Adam stopped in his tracks.

The voice was coming from behind him.

Real. And loud. As if reaching across time.

"Adam, help!"

It's Ripley's voice, you fool. Ripley, not Edgar.

Adam spun around.

"Adaaaaaaam!"

"Oh my god . . ." he murmured.

It *wasn't* over.

It was happening.

Again.